J   Lunn, Janet,
974.7   Charlotte
103
092
LUN

CHARLOTTE

CHARLOTTE

by Janet Lunn

illustrated by Brian Deines

Tundra Books

Published in Canada by Tundra Books, *McClelland & Stewart Young Readers*,
481 University Avenue, Toronto, Ontario M5G 2E9

Published in the United States by Tundra Books of Northern New York,
P.O. Box 1030, Plattsburgh, N.Y. 12901

Library of Congress Catalog Number: 96-61150

Canadian Cataloguing in Publication Data

Lunn, Janet, 1928–
            Charlotte

ISBN 0-88776-383-9

1. Haines, Charlotte, b. 1773 – Juvenile literature.
2. New York (N.Y.) – History – Revolution, 1775-1783 – Juvenile literature.
I. Deines, Brian.   II. Title.

E207. H34L86 1998   j974.7'103'092   C96-931666-6

We acknowledge the support of the Canada Council for the Arts for our publishing program.

We acknowledge the financial support of the Government of Canada through the Book
Publishing Industry Development Program for our publishing activities.

Design: Brian Bean
Printed and bound in Belgium

1 2 3 4 5 6   03 02 01 00 99 98

"Leaving? The day after tomorrow? So soon?" Charlotte's horrified whisper was so loud it reached the ears of Mistress Sewell.

"Charlotte! Elizabeth! Sarah! Return at once to your proper places. Charlotte, were your father to hear of this . . ." Mistress Sewell wrung her hands in distress.

'I know,' thought Charlotte, 'Papa would be very angry.' She gulped. Obediently she returned to her own drawing stool.

Charlotte's father and Betsy and Sally's father were both wealthy merchants in New York City. They were brothers, but they hardly spoke to each other because of the war.

It was early May in 1783, the year Charlotte Haines was ten. It was also the year thirteen rebellious American colonies won their war of independence from Great Britain after eight terrible years of fighting. Right from the start of the war, John Haines had been for the rebel cause. His brother, David, had wanted the British colonies to stay loyal to the British king. John Haines, who could not stand for anyone to disagree with him, turned his back on his brother. What's more, he forbade his whole family to have anything to do with his brother's family.

Charlotte did see Betsy and Sally, though. She saw them in church and at Mistress Sewell's Select School for Young Ladies, which they all attended six days a week. Over their tiny embroidery stitches, their careful drawings and their orderly dance steps, the cousins managed many a whispered confidence. They promised each other jolly times again when the hated war would be over.

Now they knew there would be no more jolly times together.

The war was over and all the Loyalists were to be sent into exile. Only days before Sally brought this news to school, Charlotte had overheard her father and Uncle David talking in front of her father's warehouse near the East River wharves. She had gone there with her big brother on an errand.

"So," John Haines had sneered, "you king lovers will soon be gone. General Washington only waits for your General Clinton to get the last of you Loyalists out of here. And I say we have put up with you traitors too long. It sticks in my

craw that New York has been in British hands for the entire war. Lobsterbacks everywhere you look. And refugees. Thousands of 'em. Paugh!" He shook his fist in his brother's face.

"It seems to me," said Uncle David quietly, "that you have sold as many goods as any merchant in New York City to those redcoated soldiers, and to the refugees from the other colonies."

"Be that as it may," growled John Haines. He caught sight of the children, and the conversation ended abruptly.

That evening Charlotte sat sewing by her mother's side in the parlor of the Haineses' comfortable red-brick house. Her father was standing with his back to the fire, flapping his coattails, still ranting about the Loyalists.

"Twenty British transport ships," he crowed. "Twenty of 'em, and at least two men-of-war. There are so many ships in the harbor you can scarcely see the water." He rubbed his hands together gleefully. "And all of 'em ready to take the last three thousand traitors off to the Nova Scotia wilds. Now we'll see how they feel about their dear old King George."

Charlotte cast a surreptitious look in her mother's direction. Her mother's hands were clenched in her lap. Her mouth was a grim line. Charlotte longed for her mother to say something about Betsy and Sally, but she knew her mother would dare no more than she would to disagree with John Haines.

Later, lying in her big four-poster bed, Charlotte stared up at the shadowy pattern the moonlight made on the canopy overhead.

'I could not bear to go so far from home – and to live in the wilderness!' She raised herself on one elbow and looked around at the comfortable armchair, the little worktable beside it, the settee where her dolls were arranged in a neat row, and the soft carpet on the floor. 'There will be bears and wild cats and wolves, and the Indians might be unfriendly,' she shuddered. 'Oh, how I should fear it!' She sniffed back a tear as she pictured Betsy and Sally facing all those horrors.

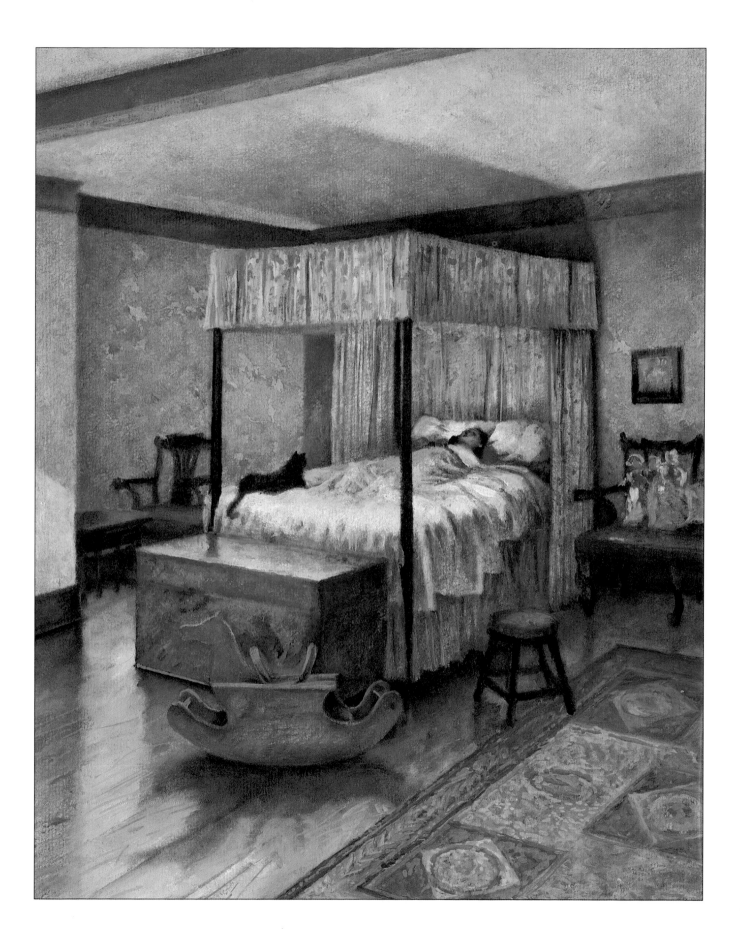

The next morning Charlotte walked, as she always did, along the cobblestone streets the few short blocks to school. She wore her flowered chintz gown over her petticoats, and had on her new red cloak and her bonnet. Now that it was spring, her mother had allowed her to wear her thin kid slippers. Phoebe, the family's young slave girl, walked a few paces behind, carrying Charlotte's books and the tightly-wrapped meat pie she would have for her noon meal.

The sun shone warm on the pansies and tulips that edged the lawns of the houses along the way, but a stiff breeze made the lilacs bounce over the iron railings. It caused the folds of Charlotte's cloak and the ribbons on her bonnet to dance and skip. Charlotte did not dance or skip. She marched resolutely along, trying not to look at the boxes and barrels, the furniture, the books and pictures piled high in the handcarts outside the houses of her Loyalist friends. All she could think was that they would be leaving in one more day. She would never see any of them again — not her friends, not her cousins — not ever again. She was almost in tears by the time she reached school. Slowly she climbed the stone steps to the big front door and stood watching Phoebe disappear back around the corner. She could not bring herself to go inside.

"I must see them once more before they go," she whispered. A lump of fear rose in her throat. Charlotte had never before defied her father. Quickly, before she could change her mind, she lifted her stiff petticoats, ran down the steps, and flew along the streets to her cousins' house.

There, too, were the handcarts piled high with all the Haineses' familiar belongings. Aunt Lucy's big old parlor clock was perched on top of the cooking pots. The house looked sad. The shutters were closed on all the windows. Charlotte pushed open the gate, hurried up the steps, and opened the door without knocking. Inside the house, all was turmoil. The smell of burnt eggs and toast filled the air. Aunt Lucy was standing in the hall. Betsy and Sally were coming down the stairs with their arms full of dolls and clothes. When the girls caught sight of Charlotte, they burst into tears.

"Charlotte, oh Charlotte," Betsy cried.

"Oh, Betsy, oh, Sally," cried Charlotte, as they rushed at each other to hug and cry and hug again until Aunt Lucy said, "Off you go, you useless baggages, and have one last cozy visit." She wiped a tear from her own eyes, gave Charlotte a quick hug, and turned back to her work.

No one said much over the noontime dinner served by red-eyed servants. Uncle David and Aunt Lucy were too preoccupied to ask Charlotte how it was that her father had allowed her to visit them. All afternoon, Uncle David bargained with dealers for what money he could get for the furniture he could not take on board ship. Aunt Lucy was stuffing whatever she could into the last packing box. Upstairs in the big feather bed, Charlotte and her cousins tried to squeeze into a few hours all the things they would never again have the chance to say to each other. Before they realized how fast those hours had sped by, it was almost supper time. Charlotte had put all thoughts of her father from her mind. Now, suddenly, she could think of nothing else. Tearfully – and fearfully – she hugged and kissed everyone for the last time and ran out the door.

The sky had turned gray and it had started to rain. Charlotte clutched her cloak tightly around her. Heedless of her thin kid slippers, she splashed through the muddy puddles.

"Dear Father in Heaven," she prayed, "let Papa be not at home. Let him be off at the tavern with his political friends. I'll sneak in through the kitchen. He'll not know I have been gone so long. Phoebe will help me."

But when she reached her own front gate, there was her father. He was standing with his arms crossed, his back to the front door. Charlotte's heart jumped with terror. She stopped.

"Where have you been?" growled her father.

"I . . . I . . ." Charlotte shuddered. 'I won't tell him,' she thought frantically. 'I'll say . . . I'll say I dawdled on the way from school.' But when she opened her mouth, to her horror, she blurted out, "I have been to see my cousins. They . . . they are to sail away tomorrow and . . ."

"And you decided to disobey your father. You decided to go against my express orders. Charlotte," he roared, "I will not countenance disobedience."

"But, Papa, I will never see them again and I had to bid them farewell. I –"

"Charlotte Haines, you are a traitor. You are just like your uncle and your aunt and your precious cousins." John Haines's voice became frighteningly quiet. "Well, Miss, you may bid farewell to your father, for you will never enter this house again."

Charlotte shrank from him as from a physical blow. "Papa," she gasped and then stopped. She could not think. The rain had penetrated her cloak and wet her gown. It had thoroughly soaked through her slippers. She scarcely noticed.

"P . . . please, Papa," her voice quavered. Hot tears stung her eyes. She took a hesitant step towards him.

"Go." He put out a hand to stop her.

"No, Papa, you cannot mean –"

"Go," he thundered, "you have made your choice. I never wish to see your traitorous face again."

For a long moment Charlotte stood there, shaking with fear and shock. Her father said nothing. He did not move. Finally, she turned and stumbled back the way she had come.

Uncle David and Aunt Lucy were horrified. Aunt Lucy held Charlotte close in her arms. Betsy and Sally found her a dry gown, and Susan, the house slave, clucking like a hen, took her slippers to dry by the kitchen fire. The only thing that made Charlotte feel any better at all was Uncle David saying, "When he's had an hour or two to calm down, I'll go to your father – if he has not already come or sent for you."

Uncle David did go to see his brother, but it did no good.

"He would not listen," Uncle David said, shaking his head sadly. "He was ever a stubborn body, man and boy alike."

"My mama?" Charlotte whispered.

"You know your mother would not go against your father, no matter how it grieved her." He drew Charlotte into his arms. "You must be our daughter now." And Charlotte knew he meant it kindly, because Uncle David was a kind and loving man. But she felt no comfort. She could think only of her mother, of her brother, and even of her father.

The next day was the bleakest day Charlotte Haines ever remembered.
Even when she was a very old lady looking back over a life that had never
again been an easy one, she could not remember a day more dreadful. Clinging
tightly to Aunt Lucy's hand, she was in a daze. The shipping wharves were
teeming with people, handcarts, and carriages. The stink of unwashed bodies,
of tar and dead fish, was everywhere. Hawkers shouted out, "Oranges, pies,
roasted chestnuts for sale." Last-minute dealers were trying to buy cheaply
whatever the refugees could not get on board ship.

And over the shouting, the calling, the sobbing farewells of families and friends were the sounds of drums and trumpets of the redcoated British soldiers leading the way to the ships – the transports and the men-of-war lying at anchor.

Like sheep following their shepherd, the refugees followed the soldiers on board, some to waste no time securing their berths below deck, others to stand by the ship's rail for the last possible sight of friends and relatives, and the city that had been their home.

While Uncle David and her cousins went below, Charlotte and Aunt Lucy stayed among those at the ship's rail, scanning the crowds, hoping for a sight of Charlotte's mother. But Charlotte's mother was not there. At last, Aunt Lucy went below deck to settle the rest of the family. Charlotte would not leave her place. She stood forlorn as the wind filled the great sails and the ship pulled away from the wharf. She stood there long after most of the other people had gone, to watch the church spires of her city fade away. She stood there until the ship had sailed through the narrows and out to sea. She stood there until Aunt Lucy came to take her to join the others. She never saw New York or anyone in her own family again.

Ten days later, the three thousand refugees were landed on the rocky shore of the Saint John harbor in the Nova Scotia wilderness. There was nothing there but a small fort, a trading post, and the tents of the refugees who had already been landed.

Eager to put the unhappy past behind them, the Loyalists were not idle. Within a year, the camp at the mouth of the Saint John River was a settlement

of log cabins and was fast becoming the town that would one day be the city of
Saint John. There were so many Loyalist refugees that by summer, in the year
after the landing at Saint John harbor, the territory north and west of the
Chignecto Isthmus was carved out of the Province of Nova Scotia to become
the new Province of New Brunswick.

Afterword

Charlotte Haines grew up along the Saint John River and became a hardworking, cheerful woman. When she was seventeen, she married a fellow Loyalist named William Peters. Charlotte and William had fifteen children and one hundred and eleven grandchildren. One of their grandchildren was Sir Samuel Leonard Tilley who became premier of New Brunswick in 1861 and one of the Fathers of Confederation in 1867.

Charlotte was a loving mother and grandmother. She was a friend to everyone who came to her home. Throughout all her long life — and she lived to be seventy-eight years old — no one ever said of Charlotte Haines Peters that she ever turned anyone away from her door.